You Are Wonderful!

Inspiring Short Stories for Girls About
Mindfulness, Courage, Love and Strength
(Great Present for Girls)

AVIA JOYCE

Thank you for buying our book!

If you find this storybook fun and useful, I would be very grateful if you could post a short review on Amazon! Your support does make a difference and I read every review personally.

If you would like to leave a review, just head on over to this book's Amazon page and click "Write a customer review".

Thank you for your support!

Table of Contents

Bright and Early

Lanie awoke bright and early on Monday morning, ready to face the week ahead of her with energy and confidence. She was especially excited because she knew that right after school that day, the basketball team would be holding tryouts. She'd been practicing dribbling the ball and her jump shot for weeks. She was sure that she'd make a great addition to the team this season.

Lanie quickly got dressed in her joggers and her favorite green sweatshirt. She then tied her basketball shoes tight and made her way out the front door and to the bus stop.

As she neared the bus stop, Lanie saw that Albert was already standing on the corner.

"Oh no," Lanie thought to herself, "there's Albert."

Lanie was sure that Albert would have something unkind to say about the basketball tryouts. Although Albert often had rude or negative things to say, Lanie tried not to let it bother her. She knew that she could do anything she set her mind to, even if Albert didn't think so.

"Hi, Albert!" Lanie greeted him brightly, trying to start the morning on a happy note.

"Hey there, Lanie. I see you've got your basketball shoes on," Albert said with a smirk.

"Yep! Tryouts are today after school," replied Lanie.

"And you're trying out?" questioned Albert. "You're not even five feet tall!"

Lanie knew he'd say something like that. Instead of getting upset, she took a deep breath and thought to herself: "I can do anything I set my mind to."

Lanie exhaled before responding.

"Nope. I'm 4'11 and I've been practicing. I can almost always sink a basket from the free throw lines," she said confidently.

"Sure you can," Albert said with some sarcasm in his voice. "Good luck."

"Thanks!" Lanie responded as the bus pulled up, determined to stay positive.

The day passed quickly for Lanie. When the final bell rang, she dashed to the gym for tryouts. She handled the ball like a pro, catching and passing and shooting, until the coach's final whistle blew.

"Looking good out there, Lanie!" the coach said. "I think we've got a spot just for you on the team this season."

Lanie was so excited! She had been so sure that she

could do this, and she was right!

That night, she fell asleep with images of winning games, three-point shots playing over and over in her head.

Lanie awoke bright and early on Tuesday morning. Lanie had a big science exam later that day. Science wasn't an easy subject for Lanie, but she'd been studying for the test for days. She was sure she'd pass the test with flying colors.

Lanie took one last peek at the planets in the solar system, stuffed her science book in her backpack, and headed out to the bus stop.

There was Albert again, already waiting for the bus.

"Hi, Albert!" Lanie chirped in a friendly voice.

"Hey there, Lanie. Ready for the big science test today? Science is pretty tough. You think you have it figured out?" Albert teased.

"I think I do," said Lanie. "I've been studying hard."

"I don't think all the studying in the world is gonna help you with this one," Albert replied.

Lanie knew he'd say something like that. Instead of getting upset, she took a deep breath and thought to herself: "I can do anything I set my mind to."

Lanie exhaled before responding.

"I'm prepared and I'm going to do great!" Lanie responded with confidence.

"Whatever you say, Lanie. Whatever you say," Albert scoffed.

"Thanks, Albert. And good luck on the test," Lanie said sincerely before, once again, stepping onto the bus.

Science was the very first subject of the day. Lanie's teacher, Mrs. Childs, passed out the exams as soon as the bell rang. Lanie felt a little nervous, but once she got started, the nerves quickly faded. She was able to answer all of the questions on the test quickly and easily. Her studying had paid off!

Mrs. Childs had the tests graded before the end of the day. Lanie was excited to see that she had gotten an A! She'd been so certain that she'd do well on the test, and she had!

That night, Lanie dreamed of all the planets in the solar system, as well as the twinkling stars and the glowing moon.

She awoke bright and early on Wednesday morning. It was the day of the big art show, and Lanie had planned on entering a painting of a purple unicorn. After adding one more layer of glitter and showing it to her mother one last time, Lanie headed out.

Of course, Albert was already waiting at the bus stop

as Lanie slowly made her way there with the painting.

"Good morning, Albert!" Lanie said happily.

"Well, well, well, what do we have here?" Albert asked as he eyed Lanie's painting.

"It's my painting for the art show. Do you like it?" asked Lanie, already knowing what his answer would be.

"It's made up. Unicorns aren't even real. I don't know how you expect to do any good with that thing," Albert pestered.

Lanie knew he'd say something like that. Instead of getting upset, she took a deep breath and thought to herself: "I can do anything I set my mind to."

Lanie exhaled before responding.

"It's alright if I don't win. I had lots of fun painting it, and it's kind of exciting just to be part of the show," said Lanie.

"Yeah, it's really exciting not to win," said Albert.

"It's fun either way. I hope you enjoy the art show," Lanie responded before hopping on the bus.

After lunch, the whole school gathered in the auditorium to look at all of the different art exhibits featured in the show. There were so many amazing things to look at. The first-place ribbon went to a clay sculpture of a Tyrannosaurus Rex. Lanie was pleasantly surprised to see that her painting had gotten sixth place in the show! Lanie was sure that she'd have fun at the show, and she'd been right!

As soon as she got home that afternoon, Lanie's father helped her hang the painting in her bedroom with the sixth-place ribbon displayed right next to it. Lanie drifted off to sleep that night while staring at the unicorn's lovely glittering mane.

Lanie awoke bright and early on Thursday morning. She drank a hot cup of tea with her oatmeal that morning to help warm up her singing voice. The school choir had a concert that evening and Lanie was going to sing a few lines of one of the songs all by herself! She had been thrilled when Mrs. Childs had picked her for such an important job.

As Lanie sipped the last of her tea staring out of the kitchen window, she could already see Albert standing at the bus stop.

"Here we go again," thought Lanie as she headed in his direction.

"Hi there, Albert!" Lanie said cheerily.

"Look! It's La-la-la-Lanie!" Albert said in a sing-song voice. "Are you ready for your big moment on stage?"

'I'm looking forward to it!' Lanie answered genuinely.

"Me too! I'm looking forward to seeing you mess up!" Albert laughed.

Lanie knew he'd say something like that. Instead of getting upset, she took a deep breath and thought to herself: "I can do anything I set my mind to."

Lanie exhaled before responding.

"Oh, I don't think I'll mess up. And, even if I do, it's no big deal. I'm still going to have fun. I hope you have fun too," Lanie answered before disappearing onto the bus.

Lanie did have fun that night. She sang every note just as she'd planned, and she sounded wonderful doing it! Lanie had been certain that she'd be able to sing all by herself, and she'd been right!

As she lay in bed after the concert, the tune ran through her head over and over until she finally fell asleep.

Lanie awoke bright and early on Friday morning. It had been a busy week, full of many exciting accomplishments. As good as a week as it had been, Lanie was getting a little tired of Albert and all of his smart remarks. She was glad it was Friday, and she was looking forward to a little break from him over the weekend.

After breakfast, she hugged her mom and dad goodbye and made the final trip to the bus stop for the week.

Just like every other morning, there was Albert.

"Happy Friday, Albert!" Lanie said, still determined to be positive and kind.

"Hi Lanie," Albert replied.

Lanie waited for more. She knew that he was going to have something to say about her jacket, or her lunchbox, or the book report that was due that afternoon. But Albert was silent.

"Are you okay, Albert?" Lanie asked, feeling a little concerned.

"Yeah, I'm alright," he said quietly.

"You don't seem alright," Lanie said softly.

"I guess I just feel kind of bad," Albert replied.

"Why?" asked Lanie.

"I've really been giving you a hard time lately. You don't deserve it," Albert said.

Lanie was shocked.

"I want to apologize," Albert continued. "You're really amazing. You made the basketball team, you did great on your science test, you got a ribbon in the art show, you sang by yourself in the choir concert—and that was just this week. Besides all that, you're always nice to me, even when I'm not very nice to you."

"It's alright, Albert. We all have rough days

sometimes. I forgive you," Lanie said.

"Thanks, Lanie. I wish I could do some of the stuff that you do," Albert said.

"There's no reason that you can't. Just tell yourself, 'I can do anything that I set my mind to'. Guess what? You can!" encouraged Lanie.

"Really?" questioned Albert.

"Sure!" said Lanie "Monday will be here before we know it! Next week will be a fresh start for both of us. We'll do it together. I'll meet you here at the bus stop— bright and early!"

City Versus Country

Delilah and Daisy were cousins and very good friends. As young girls, they had done everything together. They would spend long afternoons running and playing in sunny fields while enjoying the peaceful countryside. Sometimes at night, they would sneak off to the lights of the big city. There were lots of people and loud noises in the city, and there was always a new adventure.

As the years passed, the cousins remained close friends but chose very different lives.

Having always enjoyed those sunny days spent in the countryside, Daisy made her home in a cozy cottage deep in the country. Delilah had always loved the excitement of their nights in the city, and she built a big fancy house right in the middle of the city. Because they lived so far apart, they only got to see each other every once in a while.

One day, Delilah received a letter from her cousin Daisy. The letter spoke of their days spent in the sun-drenched fields and ended with an invitation for Delilah to visit Daisy at her cozy, country home.

Excited by the invitation, Delilah made plans to visit

right away! She packed her fancy bags and drove her very shiny, very sparkly car for many miles, over hills, and through valleys until she, at last, reached her cousin's home.

When Delilah arrived, the cousins were so happy to see one another. Daisy invited Delilah inside her tiny little cottage, which was surrounded by wildflowers and a trickling stream.

When Delilah entered the house, she was very surprised. It looked quite different from her home in the city.

"Where is your robot butler?" Delilah asked her cousin.

"I don't have one. But please come in. I'll take your coat myself, then I'll make you a tasty meal," said Daisy.

"Where is your chef?" inquired Delilah.

"I do all of my own cooking. I can make you whatever you want," replied Daisy.

Delilah was quite hungry, and she happily requested hamburgers and french fries.

After the food was prepared, Daisy called Delilah for dinner. Delilah was shocked when she saw the humble wooden table, plain clay dishes, and the worn chairs.

"This is your dining hall?" asked Delilah with some disappointment in her voice.

"I wouldn't exactly call it a dining hall, just a nice place to eat," said Daisy.

Once she sat down, Delilah found the chairs to be quite comfortable, and the food was delicious, even if it wasn't served on silver platters.

As the cousins were getting ready for bed that evening, Delilah had a wonderful idea.

"Well cousin," said Delilah, "this has been a delightful visit, but now it's my turn to treat you. You shall return to the city with me for a visit tomorrow!"

Daisy was happy to accept the invitation, as she rarely had the opportunity to travel to the city.

The next morning the two cousins awoke early. Together they drove back over the hills and through the valleys in the very shiny, very sparkly car until at last, they reached the city.

Daisy was shocked at the sight of her cousin's home. She had only seen houses like this in the movies. It was huge with an enormous ivory door, flanked with spiral-shaped bushes on each side. Right in the middle of the driveway was a sputtering, three-tiered fountain.

Delilah was excited to show Daisy her beautiful place. She eagerly turned the knob on the front door. The door was locked. It seemed strange to Daisy that someone should lock their door, for she rarely locked her own door, given the safety of her private country home.

"Oh, I know why the door is locked," said Delilah. "I do have a robot butler, and he takes excellent care of the home. He always makes sure we are safe by locking all of the doors. Let me just call him and he'll let us in."

Daisy was interested to see exactly what a robot butler might look like.

Delilah pulled out a small remote to send a message to the butler. She pressed button after button, but no one ever came to the door. Delilah soon realized that there was no battery power left in the remote. The robot butler was not receiving the signal and would not be coming to unlock the door. The cousins had no way to get inside.

Daisy soon spotted a high window that was opened just a crack. Living in the country, Daisy was used to climbing tall trees and squeezing under fences.

"Look up there!" said Daisy. "I can get us in!"

She easily made it up to the window, through the small opening, and into the house. She then skipped down the stairs to unlock the front door for Delilah.

Once the cousins were safe inside, Delilah searched for her robot butler.

"Where is he? Who shall take our things?" questioned Delilah.

She soon found him slumped in a corner, also low on battery power.

"Oh no! He's not been charging! I don't know how we'll get our things upstairs without him!" exclaimed Delilah.

Daisy was used to taking care of her own belongings, and promptly took both sets of bags upstairs.

When Daisy returned back downstairs, Delilah graciously offered dinner.

"It has been a long trip, and you have been so kind to unlock the door and put away our bags. What would you like to eat? Anything at all! My chef is happy to make it!"

Remembering the tasty hamburgers and french fries from the night before, Daisy made the same request.

"Perfect!" said Delilah. "I will tell the chef."

When the chef heard that the two cousins wanted hamburgers and french fries, he was very upset.

"I am a classically trained chef! I have worked at the finest restaurants in the world! I will not make french fries. You shall have poached quail feet!"

The cousins left the kitchen disappointed and hungry. Daisy had never tried poached quail feet, and she wasn't sure that she wanted to. Still, Delilah led them to a grand dining hall, assuring her cousin that all would be fine.

A room such as the grand dining hall was also unfamiliar to Daisy. It was huge, with fine art on the walls and marble statues in the corners. At the center of the room was a very long table, with large high-back chairs at each end.

When the two cousins were seated, they were so far apart, they had to yell at one another to be heard. The chairs were beautiful, but they were so uncomfortable that Daisy found it much more pleasant to sit on the floor. She moved her fancy silver plate to the space on the floor close to her cousin. Delilah, feeling quite uncomfortable in the chair herself, joined her cousin on the floor.

The chef soon entered the large room with a silver platter of quail feet resting on a bed of something green and gooey. Upon seeing the cousins on the floor he was, once again, angry.

"I will not serve my food on the floor! Why, the dogs have better manners than you! I'd be better off feeding them," he exclaimed with a huff as he took the food away.

Daisy was relieved at not having to eat the gooey-looking quail feet, but Delilah was very disappointed. Her cousin had been such a lovely host. She had only wanted to return the favor.

"I am sorry about our visit. I had such a nice time in

your home. I wanted to show you my home, too. Instead, we've just had one problem after another," said Delilah sadly.

"Oh, dear cousin," said Daisy, "don't you know that it isn't fancy houses or expensive things that make our time together so special? It is simply you and me."

"You are right. City or country, we will always be cousins," said Delilah, feeling less disappointed.

"And friends!" added Daisy.

"Now cousin," continued Delilah, "living in the city does have some advantages! Are you still hungry?"

"Absolutely!" answered Daisy, her stomach grumbling loudly.

With that, Daisy and Delilah returned to the very shiny, very sparkly car and drove just down the block for a hamburger and french fries.

Cloud Gazing

It was a perfect spring afternoon. The sun was shining, and a gentle breeze blew lightly through Maria's long, dark ponytail. She was lying on a checkered blanket that she'd spread out on top of the soft, green grass in her backyard. She looked up at the impossibly fluffy, white clouds in the sky above her.

Maria loved to look up at the clouds. They made her feel like anything was possible. The clouds were constantly changing and moving and growing. More than anything, Maria wanted to be just like those clouds.

As Maria gazed upward, she noticed a cloud that reminded her of a horse. It started out fuzzy and very small. As the winds shifted, the image of the horse became clearer to Maria and began to grow larger. Not only did it grow, but it appeared to be getting stronger. Maria was sure she could see the outline of big muscles in the horse's solid body. Suddenly, the horse reared up on its back legs, kicking its front legs majestically into the air. Oh, how Maria wished she had the strength of that horse!

Within seconds, the clouds changed again. This time

Maria could see a small figure on the horse's back. She rubbed her eyes. It was her! She was riding the mighty horse across the sky, as strong as any warrior that ever existed!

As she continued to stare up in amazement, Maria heard a soft rasping in the wind.

"You are strong, Maria," the wind whispered gently.

In that moment, Maria flexed her own muscles, feeling very strong indeed.

Maria continued to scan the sky overhead. The next cloud she noticed reminded her of a graceful ballet dancer. The cloud danced nimbly about the sky, appearing to extend its arm or lift one leg high into the air. Maria thought how wonderful it would be to move so gracefully.

As Maria watched, the cloud leaped this way and that, and she noticed that the features on the face of the ballet dancer began to take shape. The eyes looked a lot like her eyes, and the nose looked a lot like her nose. It was her! She was the graceful ballet dancer soaring through the clouds.

Once again, Maria heard the soft rasping in the wind.

"You are graceful, Maria," the wind gently whispered.

Maria raised her arms high above her head, showing that she was just as graceful as the ballet dancer in the sky.

As Maria lowered her arms, she noticed a new cloud forming above her. It started out as a big blob, but as the wind blew, it quickly began to take shape.

Maria was amused to find that it was taking on the form of a wise old owl, complete with round glasses sitting atop its little beak. The owl looked so clever and knowing as it observed the world around it. Maria wondered what amazing thoughts the owl must be thinking.

Maria wasn't sure, but as the cloud transformed, she thought she could see a long, dark ponytail falling down the owl's back—just like her long, dark ponytail. Could it be? Was she the wise owl? Perhaps she was. She came up with some pretty amazing thoughts herself, sometimes!

The soft rasping whistled through the air again.

"You are wise, Maria," the wind gently whispered.

Maria smiled to herself as she pretended to push a round pair of glasses over her nose. She waved goodbye to the wise owl as the clouds continued to shift.

The next cloud that caught Maria's attention was very big and shot straight up into the sky, farther than Maria could even see. Before long, the cloud started to spread out wide from side to side too. It looked to Maria like it was a tree, standing straight and tall as it extended its long branches out to either side.

Maria thought how confident the tree looked, rising

so straight and tall. Maria continued to watch the tree as a small figure appeared, standing tall in the towering limbs. It was her, just as confident and tall as the limbs she was standing among!

As the wind rustled the leaves on the cloud-tree, it carried with it the magical rasping.

"You are confident, Maria," the wind gently whispered.

Marie stretched her arms wide on each side of her body, just as sure and as steady as the oldest tree in the forest. She wiggled her fingertips as the wind blew, once more shifting the clouds in the sky above.

This cloud was a little smaller and it was even higher than all of the other clouds. As the cloud climbed higher and higher, Maria noticed that it had taken the shape of an eagle. She could see the individual feathers of its wings rustle as it soared through the air. The eagle swooped through the sky, diving and flipping without fear.

How brave the eagle was! It feared nothing as it flew just inches from the sun. As the eagle dove closer to the earth, Maria could see an even smaller cloud flying right alongside the great bird. She didn't even have to look twice this time. She knew it was her, flying just as high and as brave as the eagle. How marvelous to be unafraid, flying side by side with an eagle!

Again, came the wonderful rasping in the air.

"You are fearless, Maria," the wind whispered gently.

Maria dove into the tall grass in her backyard, ending with a spectacular forward roll. She almost felt like she was truly flying, just as brave as the girl in the clouds.

Maria landed on her back, the perfect spot to continue looking towards the sky. A low, wide cloud caught her eye. She watched as it began to take the shape of a twirling and curling vine. Growing on the vine were the plumpest, juiciest strawberries that Maria had ever seen, just waiting to be picked.

Maria thought how generous the vine was. It worked so hard to produce the small berries, and then joyfully offered them to anyone who was close enough to pick them. As Maria was wondering who might pick the strawberries in the clouds, she saw a figure take shape among the vines.

Of course, it was her! She plucked each berry from the vine and dropped it into a basket, thankful for the generosity of the plant. Maria hoped to be as giving and kind as the vine.

As she was thinking of ways that she, too, could be generous, the rasping echoed through the air.

"You are giving and kind, Maria," the wind gently whispered.

Maria thought about how she always shared her snacks with her friends, and how she was happy to lend a hand to anyone who needed help. The wind was right. She was giving and kind.

Maria looked toward the sky once again. She had been gazing at the clouds for a long time. It was becoming difficult for her to make out any more shapes among the cottony puffs. She was growing very tired. Her eyelids fluttered a few times as she tried to stay awake just a little longer. She'd been having such a lovely time. She hated to think of missing out on any of the magical clouds.

She watched a few minutes longer as the wind softly blew, continuing to shift the sky above.

This time, the rasping wind almost sounded like a lullaby as Maria slowly closed her eyes.

"You are amazing in every way, Maria," the wind whispered gently.

Maria smiled, knowing the wind's words were true, as she drifted off to sleep under billowing, white clouds.

Gotcha!

Tyla was a very thoughtful sister to her brother, Jasper, and a very thoughtful daughter to her parents.

She was always trying to think of ways to help out or make her family feel special.

Sometimes, she would feed the fish, even when it was Jasper's turn.

Sometimes, she would take the dirty laundry downstairs to the laundry room for her mother without even being asked.

Sometimes, she would have a special plate of chocolate chip cookies waiting for her father when he returned home after a long day at work.

Tyla wasn't just thoughtful when it came to her family, she was also very kind to her friends and teachers at school.

All of the kids in Tyla's class knew that they could always count on her for a kind gesture or an encouraging word.

Not only was Tyla thoughtful and kind, but she was also very clever.

One afternoon at recess, all of the kids were gathered around the slide, unsure of exactly what they wanted to do.

They were tired of swinging on the swing set.

They were tired of kickball.

They were tired of jumping rope.

All of their old games seemed boring and dull.

"Anyone want to play soccer?" asked Ben.

No one was interested.

"What about the monkey bars? We haven't climbed those in a while," suggested Taylor.

No one was interested.

"We could have a race," said Bree.

No one was interested.

All of the kids turned towards Tyla. She always seemed to come up with the best games.

"What do you think, Tyla? What game should we play?" asked Charlie.

Tyla thought for a moment.

"Hmmm," she replied, "have you ever heard of a game called Friendship Tag?"

"Not me," said Brooke.

"Me neither," said Sam.

"It's really easy to play, and fun!" Tyla said excitedly.

"How do you play?" Oliver asked.

"We start with one person whose job it is to tag all of the other kids as they try to run away. If that person tags a kid, then it's that kid's job to chase after the others and try to tag someone new," answered Tyla.

"What's so special about that?" questioned Hunter. "It just sounds like regular Tag."

"I guess it is, except for one thing," Tyla explained. "When you tag someone, you have to say something nice about them. And then when that person tags the next person, they have to say something nice about them, and so on and so on, until we've all had a turn."

"Sounds like a pretty cool game. Let's do it!" exclaimed Taylor.

"Great! I'll be the first person in charge of tagging," said Tyla. "Ready…set…go!"

As soon as Tyla had shouted the word "go!", the kids all scattered in different directions around the playground.

Tyla chased after Bree, but she was too fast.

She then set her sights on Charlie. He was just a few feet away when Tyla took off after him.

Charlie was fast, but Tyla was faster. She was able to tag him right on the shoulder just before he got away.

Tyla smiled at Charlie.

"Gotcha!" she laughed. "And...I think that you tell the best jokes! You can make anyone laugh, and you always brighten my day!"

Charlie beamed! He loved to tell jokes, but sometimes he wasn't sure that he was any good at it. It felt great to hear that Tyla thought he was funny.

Now it was Charlie's turn to chase the other kids.

At that moment, Brooke darted in front of Charlie. He ran as fast as he could, but Brooke ran fast too. Just as she was about to outrun him, his fingertips brushed her elbow.

"Gotcha!" Charlie shouted. "And...I think you're really good at math. I love how you are always willing to explain it to the rest of us, and you do a good job, too. You're a pretty good teacher for a kid!"

Brooke felt so proud. She did always make a point to explain the math homework to anyone who may not understand. She hadn't realized that the other kids appreciated it so much.

Now it was Brooke's turn to chase the other kids.

Hunter jumped towards her in a teasing way, then jumped back when Brooke lunged at him.

Brooke laughed and continued to chase Hunter as he shot across the playground. Brooke was just as fast, and was soon able to tag him right in the middle of his back.

"Gotcha!" said Brooke. "And...I think that you are really friendly. When I started as a new student at school last year, you were the first kid to sit with me at lunch. That really made me feel welcome. Thanks!"

Hunter couldn't believe that Brooke had remembered that he had sat with her that very first day at lunch. Hunter had been new the year before, and he remembered how scary being the new kid could be. He didn't want anyone else to have to feel that way.

Now it was Hunter's turn to chase the other kids.

He didn't have to chase far. Oliver was right behind him. It seemed like all that Hunter had to do was turn around and tag him on the arm.

"Gotcha!" said Hunter. "And...I think you have an awesome attitude. Whenever there is a problem to be solved, you are always confident that we can get it done, like that time we had to make a volcano in science class. Everyone else complained that we'd never get it finished on time, except you. You pushed all of us, and we did finish it."

Oliver smiled as he thought of the volcano project. He'd actually had a great time completing it with all his friends. He did always try to have a positive attitude, and share it with those around him, as well.

Now it was Oliver's turn to chase the other kids.

There was no one in sight, but that didn't bother Oliver. He knew that he'd catch someone. He rushed around the playground before practically smashing into Taylor, who was trying to run in the other direction. Too late! Oliver tagged her right in the shoulder.

"Gotcha!" said Oliver. "And...you're the most helpful kid in our class. You are always cleaning up messes that you didn't make or helping the younger kids button up their coats and put on their mittens."

Oliver's words made Taylor feel warm and happy on the inside. She tried to always help in any way that she could. It felt good for someone to notice her efforts.

Now it was Taylor's turn to chase the other kids.

The first person she saw was Sam. She took off after him, quick as a flash. Sam turned around to see Taylor right behind him and stumbled over his feet. Taylor took the opportunity to tag Sam on the wrist.

"Gotcha!" said Taylor. "And...you keep a very tidy desk, you always hand your homework in on time, and all your pencils are arranged from smallest to biggest. I wish I could be more like that."

Sam laughed! He hadn't realized that anyone had ever noticed how responsible he was. It was important for him to keep his things neat and organized. He liked being an example for his friends.

Now it was Sam's turn to chase the other kids.

He looked around and zeroed in on Bree. She hadn't been tagged yet. He chased after her and just as he was about to tag her on the top of the head, she bent down. Sam bent down too, and just barely tagged her on the ankle.

"Gotcha!" said Sam. "And...you always share everything that you have. Just last week you gave me a cupcake at lunch, you loaned Oliver some colored pencils in art class, and you brought a bottle of water to Charlie after gym class. You are the most generous person I know."

Bree always shared everything that she had. She loved how she felt when she gave something special to someone or loaned them something useful. How nice it felt for her friends to think of her as generous!

Now it was Bree's turn to chase the other kids.

Ben was one of the only kids left who hadn't been tagged. Bree saw him standing next to the flag people and dashed in his direction. He didn't have time to get away before Bree tagged him on the knee.

"Gotcha!" said Bree. "And...I think you work harder than anyone I know. You never give up, even when things are tough. Do you remember when that storm blew all of those branches and tree limbs down at the park last spring? You didn't stop picking them up until every last twig was taken care of. That was pretty amazing!

Ben did remember working hard in the park the day after the storm. He just liked to work, especially if he was doing something to help out other people. He always felt satisfied after he'd put in a hard day of work.

Now it was Ben's turn to chase the other kids.

Everyone had been tagged already. Everyone except for Tyla.

There she was, standing right by the jungle gym. Ben ran towards her. Of course, Tyla was so kind, she didn't even try to run from him. She wanted to let Ben win.

As Ben approached, Tyla gave him a warm and encouraging smile.

"Come on, Ben! You can do it!" she yelled.

Ben could hardly bring himself to tag her. The whole wonderful game had been her idea in the first place.

Tyla continued to yell: "Come and get me, Ben!"

And he did. But instead of tagging her, he gave her a great big high five.

When the others saw the playful gesture, they all lined up behind Ben. Everyone wanted a chance to give Tyla a high five.

Tyla eagerly slapped each kid's hand, feeling grateful for all of her friends and all of their special qualities.

An Important Purpose

Anna lived on a small farm with her parents and her younger brother, William. There were always lots of things to keep Anna busy on the beautiful land surrounding their home.

There were three apple trees, a cherry tree, and a pear tree in the orchard next to the barn. There were seven hens in the chicken coop. There was a small brown stream that trickled beyond the pasture. There was a cow named Murray, a dog named Roxie, and there was almost always a litter of small gray and black kittens, either darting through the barn or snuggled up in the cozy hay.

Anna loved to spend her afternoons exploring all of the wonders that the farm held. There were several small buildings dotting the land. Some were for the storage of tractors and other farm equipment, while others were shelters for the few animals on the farm.

One small white shed had never been used by the family for anything. It just stood empty on the edge of the property. The neighbors had told Anna's mother that the people who had lived in the house before Anna's family had used it as a chicken coop, but when they had moved in, Anna's father had built a brand-new chicken coop. The small white shed, with its splintered wood, peeling paint and crooked door, seemed useless.

Anna's father often talked about tearing the small building down. This always made Anna feel sad. She thought it was a shame to tear down something that had once had such an important purpose.

One evening at dinner, Anna's father, once again, brought up the subject of the small shed.

"I think I should finally be able to get around to tearing down that old shed tomorrow," he said between mouthfuls of mashed potatoes. "Once we get it cleared away, it'll be the perfect spot to plant that strawberry patch we're always talking about."

Anna felt a small flash of panic rise in her chest. She hated the thought of the shed being torn down. She could no longer contain herself.

"Dad, please don't tear it down!" she blurted out desperately.

"The shed? Why don't you want me to tear that old thing down?" he asked with some confusion.

"I can't say for sure," said Anna. "It's just that it used to be such a useful and important part of the farm. I can't imagine just tearing it down."

"Well, what do you suggest that we do with it?" asked her father.

"I don't know…" said Anna, slowly forming a plan in her mind, "maybe I could have it?"'

"You want it? What would you do with it?" her father questioned.

Anna thought for a moment.

"I'd take care of it. It would be nice to have a space all my own," Anna said.

Anna's father looked over the dinner table towards Anna's mother.

"Seems like a pretty good idea to me," said Anna's mother as she winked at Anna. "We can always plant the strawberries by the front gate."

Anna's hopes soared.

"If it's alright with everyone else, I guess it's alright with me," Anna's father replied.

Anna was so excited she could hardly finish her meal. She couldn't wait to fix up her special place.

The next morning, Anna woke up bright and early and set to work. She started by cracking open the three small compartments that had previously been used to reach into the coop to gather eggs. Once they were open, they were like little windows, letting lots of fresh air and sunshine into the shed. She then swept out the little shed.

Next, she cleared out years of dirt and dust from the old roosts and carefully removed the chicken wire. Once they were cleaned up, Anna knew that they would make perfect shelves. She finished by freshening up the peeling white paint with a fresh coat. Her mother let her use the last of the paint they had used on the kitchen windowsill earlier that spring. She examined her hard work, feeling proud of herself. She was so happy that the shed would, once more, have an important purpose.

As Anna went into the garage to put away the paintbrush, she noticed the old kitchen rug rolled up and leaning against the trash cans. Her mother must have put it there to be taken away with the garbage the next morning. Seeing it lying with all of the trash gave Anna the same feeling she had when her father had told her that he was going to tear down the shed. The rug had laid in front of the kitchen door for years. The family had always used it to wipe their feet whenever they came into the house. It seemed so sad to get rid of something that had been so useful, something that could still be useful.

She gathered the old rug up in her arms and took it out to her shed. She unrolled it and gave it a good shake before laying it down in front of her own shed door. She gently wiped her feet on the rug. She was so happy that the rug would, once more, have an important purpose.

Now that the inside was finished, Anna set about tidying the outside of the shed by pulling the long weeds that had grown up around it. As she rounded the back side of the shed, she noticed Roxie's old water dish upside down in the grass. It had been many months since Anna had seen the dish. The old silver bowl had a small dent on one side, with just a bit of rust on the bottom. Other than that, it was in perfect condition.

Once again, Anna felt a little sad. Roxie had used the dish for years, and it had always served her well. Now it lay forgotten in the tall grass. Suddenly, an idea came to Anna. She had wanted to move her rock collection out to the shed. Roxie's old bowl would be the perfect way to display them on the shelf!

She quickly cleaned out the bowl with the garden hose and shook it dry. She then took the dish inside, piled it high with the many unique rocks she had collected over the years, and carried it back out to the shed. Anna found the perfect spot to display the rocks – right next to a small set of books that she had moved out to the shed. She was so happy that the dish would, once more, have an important purpose.

There was just one problem. The books kept falling over and knocking the rocks out of the bowl. If only she had something to help keep the books in place. Surely, she could find something in the barn that might help with the problem, Anna reasoned.

She made her way to the large barn, then walked slowly through, looking for something heavy that she could use to prop up the books. In the back corner of the barn, she found a pile of metal scraps. Sitting right on top of the pile was the old yellow teakettle that had sat atop the stove since Anna was a baby. Anna remembered the last time her mother had tried to make tea with it, the spout had dribbled, spilling hot water all over the countertops. Her mother must have thrown it out here to be hauled off to the dump with the rest of the metal scraps.

There was that sad feeling again. Anna thought about how many times the kettle had been used to boil water for her morning oatmeal, and seeing it lying in the junk pile almost made her feel like crying. After staring at the kettle for a few seconds, Anna got another idea. She could use the teakettle to help prop up her books!

Anna ran back to her shed with the heavy metal kettle swinging back and forth as she gripped the handle. Once she made it back, she carefully lined up her books on the shelf. She then took the lid off the teakettle and placed it on one side of the book collection and placed the kettle on the other side. It worked! The books stood tall and straight supported by the teakettle and the lid.

She was so happy that the teakettle would, once more, have an important purpose.

Anna stepped back and looked at the shed. It was sparkling clean and filled with all sorts of rescued treasures. She felt proud, and she was eager to show off her hard work to William and her parents.

That evening, after supper, she invited the whole family out to the shed.

"Oh, Anna!" her mother exclaimed. "The fresh paint looks so nice!"

"And look at how you've cleared out all the weeds. It looks much better," her father added.

"Yeah!" said William. "I want my own shed, too."

"Wait until you see the inside!" Anna said excitedly.

She pushed open the door and they all walked inside the tiny building.

"Is that the old kitchen rug?" her father asked as he looked down.

"It sure is," said Anna proudly.

"Well, that's pretty clever," he said, wiping his feet before he entered.

"Look!" shouted William pointing to the rock collection on the shelf. "It's Roxie's old dish! Cool!"

Anna smiled.

"My teakettle!" Anna's mother gasped when she saw the bookends. "How perfect to hold up your books! It's just wonderful how you've saved all of our old things!"

"It made me a little sad to see all of it pushed to the side or thrown away. They had all had such an important purpose. I knew they still had an important purpose," Anna replied.

Anna's mother and father smiled, feeling almost as proud of Anna as she felt of her shed.

"You want to know something?" asked Anna's father. "You've had a pretty important purpose yourself this evening."

"You certainly have," laughed Anna's mother. "I guess we'll all think twice before we throw out any more treasures."

"That's right! And, now for the most special treasure of all!" said Anna, as she placed a framed picture of the whole family right next to Roxie's bowl.

mighty Molly

Molly was little, but she was very mighty.

She always tried her very best, but sometimes things were just a little harder for Molly.

This didn't bother Molly. She knew that she was still mighty.

Molly wasn't as strong as her brother Miles.

Miles could carry three bags of groceries in from the car, while Molly could only carry one.

Even if she wasn't as strong as Miles, Molly knew that she was still mighty.

She wasn't as tall as her cousin Keira.

Keira could reach the apples growing on the tallest branches of the apple tree, while Molly could only reach the apples growing on the branches hanging close to the ground.

Even if she wasn't as tall as Keira, Molly knew that she was still mighty.

She wasn't as fast as her friend Charlotte.

Charlotte could always beat her big dog Buster in a

race, while Molly could barely keep up with her tiny dog Daisy.

Even if she wasn't as fast as Charlotte, Molly knew that she was still mighty.

Molly wasn't able to jump as high as her sister Deena.

Deena could jump rope higher than anyone in the whole park. She would jump and jump and jump for what seemed like hours, while Molly could only spin the rope a few times beneath her before getting tangled up.

Even if she couldn't jump as high as Deena, Molly knew that she was still mighty.

`Tyler zipped through one book after another during reading time, sometimes reading three or four books in one day, while Molly took her time with each new book, usually just reading one book a day.

Even though she didn't read as fast as Tyler, Molly knew that she was still mighty.

Molly wasn't as outgoing as her neighbor Lucy.

Lucy could easily talk with anyone and make lots of new friends, while Molly was a little shy and meeting new people could sometimes make her a bit nervous.

Even if she wasn't as outgoing as Lucy, Molly knew that she was still mighty.

Molly wasn't as good of an artist as her friend Danny.

Danny could paint almost anything – he painted the best dogs and rabbits in minutes, while it took Molly an hour just to paint a rainbow.

Even though Molly may not have been as good of an artist as Danny, she knew that she was still mighty.

No, Molly may not have always been the fastest, or the strongest, or the tallest, but Molly was still very, very mighty.

When Miles brought his three bags of groceries into the kitchen, he dropped the eggs and spilled the milk. He put the potatoes in the bread box and the bread in the potato bin. The kitchen was always a mess when Miles had finished putting away the groceries.

When Molly brought her one bag of groceries into the kitchen, she neatly placed the butter in the butter dish and arranged the pears in the fruit bowl. She always made sure all of the drawers and cabinets were closed behind her. The kitchen always sparkled when Molly had finished putting away the groceries.

When Keira picked apples from the tallest branches on the apple tree, she usually only picked three: one to eat right away, one to eat after supper, and one to eat the next morning. Keira wasn't very thoughtful when it came to picking apples.

When Molly picked apples from the low-hanging

branches, she picked a whole bushel basket full. She always picked plenty of apples for Miles, and some for her mom and dad, too. She picked lots of extra apples so that she could make an apple pie with her grandmother. Molly was very thoughtful when it came to picking apples.

When Charlotte raced her dog Buster, she was usually so tired afterward that she collapsed right in the grass, forgetting all about Buster. She would then hurry off to fill up her water bottle after the long, hot race. Charlotte didn't pay much attention to Buster once the race was over.

When Molly raced her dog Daisy, she always checked on Daisy afterward to make sure she wasn't too hot or too tired. When Molly filled up her water bottle, she made sure to grab Daisy's water dish and fill it up too. Molly always took good care of Daisy when the race was over.

When Deena jumped rope at the park, she would use the jump rope for hours and hours. She loved jumping so much that she hardly ever let anyone else have a turn with the jump rope. Deena was a little selfish with the jump rope.

When Molly jumped rope at the park, she would always share her jump rope with anyone who wanted a turn. She was always happy to share the jump rope with all of the younger kids, and some of the older ones too. Molly was very generous with the jump rope.

When Tyler read his books during reading time, he usually couldn't remember what he'd read about. Sometimes, he just wanted to be the fastest reader in the class. Tyler didn't always learn new things from the books that he had read.

When Molly read her books during reading time, she took her time and really paid attention to what she was reading. She enjoyed reading and she would sometimes read the same parts two or three times, just to make sure that she understood. Molly always learned new things from the books that she had read.

When Lucy met new people, she talked and talked and talked. Sometimes, Lucy wouldn't even give others the chance to talk. If they did have a chance to talk, Lucy didn't always listen, or she would interrupt. Lucy had a hard time taking turns and listening to others.

When Molly met new people, she always let them do plenty of talking. She asked lots of questions and she was interested in what they had to say. Molly was very good at listening to others and waiting her turn to talk.

When Danny painted, he often became frustrated if the painting got difficult. If he was trying to paint something new, sometimes he would give up, or just go back to painting dogs and rabbits. Danny gave up easily when things got hard.

When Molly painted, she tried her very best every single time. She liked painting new things, and she never gave up, even if it was a little tricky.

Molly never gave up when things got hard.

No, Molly may not have been as strong as Miles.

Or as tall as Keira.

Or as fast as Charlotte.

And she may not have been able to jump as high as Deena.

Or read as fast as Tyler.

Or make friends as easily as Lucy.

Or paint as well as Danny.

But she was…

Responsible

And thoughtful

And caring

And generous

And smart

And polite

And determined.

And these things made Molly very mighty, indeed!

Sadie's Secrets

Sadie loved to help others.

She helped her sister, her friends, and her parents. She even helped her dog, Bubbles, sometimes.

Whenever she saw someone who was feeling lonely or sad or worried, she knew just how she could help.

Sadie would simply whisper a magical secret in their ear and, in no time at all, they would be feeling much better.

One afternoon, as Sadie was taking Bubbles for a walk, she noticed that her sister Meg was sitting on the edge of the playground all by herself. Sadie could tell that Meg was feeling unhappy as she plopped down next to her.

"What's wrong, Meg?" Sadie asked gently.

Meg stared at all of the other children playing together on the playground for several seconds before answering.

"Everyone has a friend but me. Tyler and Jack are playing baseball together. Caroline and Beth are jumping rope together. William and Liv are swinging together. I'm just sitting here, all by myself," answered Meg sadly.

Sadie didn't like her sister feeling lonely. She thought

for a moment.

"Meg, can I tell you a secret?" asked Sadie.

"I guess," said Meg, still feeling quite sad.

Sadie leaned in close to Meg's ear.

"I know of a magical place. It's a place full of friends. There are big friends and little friends. The trees and flowers are friends. The sunshine and the moonshine are friends. Even the snakes and the spiders are friends. Everywhere you look, there is another friend!" Sadie told Meg excitedly.

"Sounds like an amazing place!" said Meg dreamily.

"If there is such a place like this, full of friends for everyone, then certainly you can make one friend too!" said Sadie.

Meg thought for a moment, beginning to feel a little better, as she glanced around the playground hopefully.

"Go on," encouraged Sadie. "There is an open swing right next to Beth."

"Thanks, Sadie!" said Meg before rising from her spot on the edge of the playground.

Still thinking about the magical land of friendship, she made her way over to the swings.

It wasn't long before Beth, Caroline, and Meg were all laughing together as they swung high into the air.

Sadie watched her sister for a moment, happy that she had new friends, before turning her attention to the tall, tall slide.

There, standing at the bottom of the ladder, was her friend Leo.

His head was tilted back, chin raised towards the sky, as he looked towards the top of the slide.

Sadie walked over to her friend.

"Hi Leo!" she said cheerily. "Are you going to go down the slide?"

Leo continued to look up doubtfully.

"I don't know. I really, really want to, but it's pretty high up. The slide is at least as tall as a giraffe, maybe even a T-Rex," said Leo.

Sadie could tell that Leo was feeling a little scared. She thought for a moment.

"Leo, can I tell you a secret?" asked Sadie.

"Yeah," Leo answered quietly.

Sadie leaned in close to Leo's ear.

"I know of a magical place. Everyone there is very brave. They jump from cloud to cloud. They ride on the backs of the fastest unicorns, and they slide all the way from the top of the rainbow down to the bottom," Sadie told Leo excitedly.

"All the way down the rainbow?" Leo asked in awe.

"All the way down," said Sadie. "If there is such a place as this, full of people bravely trying new things, then certainly you can go down that slide, too."

Leo tilted his head upward again – this time, more confidently.

"You can do it, Leo!" Sadie encouraged.

"Thanks, Sadie! I can do it!" said Leo.

As he climbed each rung of the ladder, Leo thought about the clouds and the unicorns and the rainbow slide until he finally made it to the top. Sadie watched for a moment as Leo gleefully raced down the slide.

Just as she was turning away, she noticed her mother on a nearby park bench, digging through her bag with a frown on her face.

"Hi, Mom. What's wrong?" asked Sadie as she approached.

"Oh, I can't find my silly sunglasses! I'm always misplacing them," her mother replied impatiently.

Sadie knew that her mother was feeling frustrated as she continued to dig through her bag, sighing heavily. She thought for a moment.

"Mom, can I tell you a secret?" asked Sadie.

"Alright but I really need to find my sunglasses,"

answered her mother.

Sadie leaned in close to her mother's ear.

"I know of a magical place. It is filled with playful fairies who hide things from the people who live there. Sometimes they hide golden coins. Other times, they hide sparkling jewels. When someone discovers that a coin or a jewel is missing, they always do the same thing. They take a deep breath, and then they calmly look around until they find it. And they always find it," Sadie told her mom excitedly.

"I think I could use some of their patience," her mother said with a tiny smile.

"If there is such a place as this, filled with people patiently finding all of their lost belongings, surely you can find just one pair of sunglasses," said Sadie.

"I can," her mother said calmly.

"Start by taking a deep breath," Sadie gently encouraged.

No sooner had her mother closed her eyes and taken a deep breath, then her eyes snapped back open.

She quickly felt the top of her head with her hands. There, hiding in the dark curls piled on top of her head, were her sunglasses!

"I found them!" her mother exclaimed. "Thank you, Sadie!"

Sadie just smiled.

"Sadie, can I tell you a secret?" asked her mother.

"Sure!" Sadie answered, excited at the thought of hearing a secret instead of telling one.

Her mother leaned in close to Sadie's ear.

"I know of a magical girl. Her heart is enormous, and she spreads kindness wherever she goes. She helps those who are feeling lonely or afraid or frustrated."

Sadie glowed at her mother's words.

"If there is such a girl as this, filled with joy and goodness, certainly she must make the world a better place," her mother said tenderly.

Beaming, Sadie thought about all of her secrets, and how this secret was her very favorite!

Strong. Brave. Smart. Important.

Tara wasn't afraid to do hard things. And there were lots of hard things that Tara had to do every day. It wasn't always easy, and it wasn't always fun, but she always got through it.

Tara knew she was strong. Tara knew she was brave. Tara knew she was smart. Tara knew she was important. Because she was sure of all of these things, Tara knew that she could do anything she set her mind to.

Sometimes, Tara did not want to get out of bed in the mornings. She still felt sleepy, and it was hard to think about crawling out of the cozy blankets. When her mother would come in and pull open her window shades, all that Tara wanted to do was hide under the covers and go back to sleep.

But she knew that wasn't what she should do.

Instead of hiding under the covers, Tara would close her eyes and repeat to herself: "I am strong, I am brave. I am smart. I am important. And I can get out of bed this morning!"

Like a flash, Tara would hop out of bed, brush her teeth, get dressed, and be on her way!

Sometimes, Tara did not want to ride the school bus. The bus could be bumpy and uncomfortable. The other kids were loud and sometimes even a little rude. When the big yellow bus pulled up in front of her house, all that Tara wanted to do was turn around and shuffle back home.

But she knew that wasn't what she should do.

Instead of shuffling back home, Tara would close her eyes and repeat to herself: "I am strong, I am brave. I am smart. I am important. And I can get on that bus!"

She would then slowly trudge up the steep school bus steps and find her seat among the other kids. Before very long at all, Tara would arrive at school, safe and sound.

Sometimes, Tara did not want to complete her spelling test. It made her stomach feel nervous and she worried about spelling the words wrong. When her teacher would announce that it was time to start the test, all that Tara wanted to do was to slide underneath the desk and take cover until it was over.

But she knew that wasn't what she should do.

Instead of sliding underneath her desk, Tara would close her eyes and repeat to herself: "I am strong, I am brave. I am smart. I am important. And I can finish this spelling test!"

As soon as Tara set to work on the test, she always did better than she thought she would. Even if she didn't get all of the answers right, it felt good to know that she was trying her hardest.

Sometimes, Tara did not want to run the half-mile race during gym class. She was far from being the fastest kid in the class, and she was worried that she might come in last place or, worse yet, stumble and fall. When she would hear the high-pitched "tweet" of her gym teacher's whistle, all she wanted to do was turn around and run back to the locker room.

But she knew that wasn't what she should do.

Instead of running back to the locker room, Tara would close her eyes and repeat to herself: "I am strong, I am brave. I am smart. I am important. And I can run the half-mile race!"

Tara would start by putting one foot in front of the other. Before she knew it, Tara would be finished with the whole half-mile! She may not always be the fastest, but she always finished!

Sometimes, Tara did not want to go to piano lessons. She didn't think she was very good at playing the piano, and there were so many other things that she would rather be doing. When it was time to start practicing the piano scales, all she wanted to do was hop up from the bench and go and watch TV.

But she knew that wasn't what she should do.

Instead of hopping up from the piano bench, Tara would close her eyes and repeat to herself: "I am strong, I am brave. I am smart. I am important. And I can play the piano!"

With that, Tara would begin plinking away on the piano. Before the lesson was over, she would even be enjoying the beautiful music she was making.

Sometimes, Tara did not want to clear the dinner table. It took forever to finish the job and it seemed to her that she always had to clear the table while her younger brother relaxed in the living room. When the family had finished the meal and her parents looked across the table at her, all that Tara wanted to do was sneak off to the living room and relax on the couch.

But she knew that wasn't what she should do.

Instead of sneaking off to the couch, Tara would close her eyes and repeat to herself: "I am strong, I am brave. I am smart. I am important. And I can clear the dinner table!"

One cleared plate would turn into two cleared plates, and then three plates, and then four plates. Pretty soon, Tara would have the entire table cleared, with plenty of time left to relax on the couch.

Sometimes, Tara did not want to finish her math homework. Math was hard for Tara. The numbers never seemed to make sense, especially when she had to subtract or multiply them. When it was time to pull out her math book, all that Tara wanted to do was slam it shut and stuff it into her backpack.

But she knew that wasn't what she should do.

Instead of slamming the book shut, Tara would close her eyes and repeat to herself: "I am strong, I am brave. I am smart. I am important. And I can figure out my math homework!"

If Tara really concentrated, the numbers would actually start to make sense to her. When she struggled with a problem, her mom and dad were always there to help. Tara felt proud after she had completed all the hard work.

Sometimes, Tara did not want to go to bed. It had been two years since Tara had slept with a nightlight, but every once in a while, she heard a strange creaking sound in the hallway. When she heard the strange sound, all that Tara wanted to do was jump out of bed and flip on all of the lights.

But she knew that wasn't what she should do.

Instead of jumping out of bed and flipping on the

lights, Tara would close her eyes and repeat to herself: "I am strong, I am brave. I am smart. I am important. And I will stay in bed!"

All it took was for Tara to remind herself how brave she was. She would then remember that the creaking in the hallway was just her cat, Freckles, walking across the old wooden floorboards. Feeling safe and secure, she would then be ready to settle down for the night.

Each night as she lay in bed, Tara would think about all of the tough things she had done throughout the day. She wasn't sure exactly when she had learned how strong, brave, smart, and important she was. She just knew that she was all of those things – and more.

Every night, just as Tara was drifting off to sleep, her mother and her father would tiptoe into her bedroom one last time to say goodnight.

And every night, Tara was so sleepy, she wouldn't even realize that they'd come in.

"Goodnight, Tara. Never forget that you are strong. Never forget that you are brave," her father would whisper as he tucked the covers underneath her chin.

"Goodnight, Tara. Never forget that you are smart. Never forget that you are important," her mother would whisper just before she gently kissed her on the forehead.

Tara would fall asleep with the words "strong", "brave", "smart", and "important" dancing through her mind. When she awoke the next morning, she'd be ready to face another day.

The Talent Show

"Talent Show In Two Weeks! Sign Up In The Lunchroom Today!" read the large, neon-green poster that hung on the front doors of the school.

As the final school bell of the day rang, Josie and her friend Dana made their way out of the building.

When Josie pushed open the heavy door the bright sign caught her eye.

"Oh, wow!" exclaimed Josie to Dana. "I've always wanted to be in a talent show!"

"You should go for it!" encouraged Dana as they bustled through the door and out into the afternoon sun. "It sounds like fun. But what would you do for your talent?"

Josie thought for a minute. She didn't really know what she might do for her talent. She just knew that she'd always wanted to be in a talent show. Even more than that, she knew that she'd always wanted to win a talent show.

The two friends sat down together on a bench outside the school to further discuss Josie's plans.

"Hmm...," said Josie. "Maybe I could juggle."

"Like with balls? Do you even know how to do that?" asked Dana.

"Nope. Maybe I should choose something else," replied Josie.

"Good idea," said Dana. "Why don't you sing?"

"I couldn't carry a tune in a bucket," teased Josie.

"True," agreed Dana. "You could dance."

"The last time I tried to dance I ended up tripping over my feet and falling flat on my face!" laughed Josie.

"That's right. At least you are a good sport about it," said Dana.

"There's got to be something I can do," Josie thought out loud.

"Ride a unicycle? Twirl a baton? Make balloon animals?" offered Dana.

"No, no, and no!" Josie giggled.

"Alright, alright. No more jokes," promised Dana. "You'll figure it out."

Suddenly, Josie popped up from the bench.

"I've got it!" she exclaimed. "I know exactly what I'm going to do for the talent show!"

"What? What?" asked Dana excitedly.

"No time to talk! I have to go practice!" called Josie as

she gathered up her backpack and rushed home, leaving her friend confused and curious.

Josie ran all the way home, excited to start working on her act for the talent show right away.

She flung open the kitchen door to find her brother Roger sitting at the table with a huge glass of milk and a peanut butter and jelly sandwich in front of him.

"What are you so worked up about?" asked Roger, noticing how excited Josie was.

"The talent show! I'm going to sign up for the talent show," said Josie.

"Yeah right," groaned Roger. "What kind of talent do you have?"

"I have lots of talents," Josie said confidently. "And you're just going to have to wait and see."

"Good luck," said Roger half-heartedly before turning his attention back to his sandwich.

Josie didn't let Roger's lack of confidence bother her. She knew exactly what she was going to do, and she was sure she would get the top prize in the show.

After grabbing a quick snack for herself, she went directly to her room and started planning her act. She was in there for what seemed like hours before her mother finally tapped on her door.

"Josie, it's almost dinner time," her mother said through the closed door. "You've been in there all evening. Come on out and eat with us."

Josie cracked open the door. "I can't come out now, Mom. I'm practicing," she insisted.

"I know. Roger told me all about the talent show. But you've got to come out sometime," replied her mother.

"Alright Mom, I'll come out for dinner, but then it's right back to practicing. I've only got two weeks!" said Josie.

Several minutes later, Josie finally joined her family at the dinner table.

"What are you doing in there, Josie? Or is it top secret?" said her father as he smiled at her over a spoonful of mashed potatoes.

"I'm practicing for the talent show," said Josie. "And it's, kind of, a surprise."

"A surprise? Now I'm really curious," her mother said.

"You'll just have to wait until the talent show," Josie said slyly.

"Can't wait!" said her father, helping himself to more mashed potatoes and turning the conversation towards other events of the day.

But Josie couldn't concentrate on anything that anyone in her family said. All she could think about was her act for the talent show. And as soon as dinner was over and the dishes were cleared from the table, Josie went right back to her room to continue her practice.

When she awoke the next morning, she dashed out the door, eager to get to school so she could sign up for the talent show.

She ran right to the lunchroom and added her name to the list of other talent show participants.

Right next to her name, Josie was supposed to write what sort of talent she would be doing in the show. Josie just wrote, "SURPRISE!"

For the next two weeks, Josie spent every spare second practicing for the show. All of her friends and her family were so curious about what Josie's surprise talent might be. She never told anyone—she just practiced and practiced and practiced and practiced!

The days flew by until the night of the big show arrived. Her mom and her dad and her friend Dana waited excitedly in the front row. Even Roger was on the edge of his seat intently waiting for Josie's act.

There were lots of kids performing in the show. Kelly sang a song. Wyatt played a solo on his guitar. Nina pulled a rabbit out of a black top hat. Josie watched from behind the curtains, impressed with all of the talent at her school.

After about six more acts, it was Josie's turn to perform. As the stage lights went dark, she took a deep breath, gathered up her props, and headed to the center of the stage.

She stood perfectly still on the darkened stage. Suddenly, the spotlight hit Josie, lighting her up and finally revealing her surprise talent.

Energetic music blared over the loud speakers as Josie slid a silver hula hoop over her head and down to her waist. Around and around went the silver hoop as Josie wiggled her body back and forth. After several seconds with the single spinning hoop, Josie carefully reached down and grabbed another hoop. While keeping the first one going, Josie slid the second one around her waist and spun two hoops at once!

After several more seconds, Josie reached for a third hoop and slipped it around her right arm. She now had three hoops going—two around her waist and one around her arm! Carefully, she slipped a fourth hoop over her left arm and spun it around. Four hoops at once!

One more silver hoop lay on the ground by Josie's feet. Carefully, carefully, with all four hoops still spinning, Josie slipped the fifth hoop over her head and around her neck. Josie moved her neck in a circle and started the final hoop spinning. Five hoops circled around Josie in time to the loud music!

Her family and her friends sat in the audience completely amazed. They had no idea that Josie had such a talent. As the final notes of the song faded over the loudspeakers, Josie stopped spinning and gracefully removed all five hoops from her body. The audience went wild, clapping and cheering for Josie's unique talent.

Josie picked up her silver hoops and hurried backstage to watch the rest of the talent show. There were still a few more acts to go before the winners were announced. Josie was sure that she would get the first prize trophy!

After a tap dance, a puppet show, and a tumbling act, it was finally time for the awards. Josie could barely contain her excitement!

The school principal, Mrs. Charles, made her way to the microphone holding a big third-place trophy, an even bigger second-place trophy, and a HUGE first-place trophy.

She tapped on the microphone before beginning. "Ladies and gentlemen, it is my pleasure to present the third-place trophy to Michael and his frisbee-catching dog, Peppermint! Come and get your trophy Michael and Peppermint!"

The crowd cheered as the pair collected their trophy.

Josie was nervous as she waited for the next name to be called.

"Our second-place trophy goes to Taylor and her beautiful piano solo!" raved Mrs. Charles.

Again, the audience clapped as Taylor received her trophy. Again, Josie sat nervously backstage waiting for her name to be called.

Mrs. Charles held up the first-place trophy. "And our final, and biggest, award goes to...Anna-Beth and her hilarious comedy routine!" the principal gushed.

The audience stood and cheered happily as all three winners proudly took a final bow. Josie, on the other hand, wasn't quite so happy. She couldn't believe that she hadn't gotten a single award, not even third place. She had worked so hard. She could feel a lump form in her throat as tears welled up in her eyes.

From her spot backstage, Josie could hear Mrs. Charles begin to speak into the microphone one more time.

"We have one more, very special award, to give this evening," said Mrs. Charles. "This award goes to the most creative act. And the winner is...Josie and her spinning silver hoops!"

Josie quickly wiped away her tears and ran out onto the stage where Mrs. Charles was waiting with a huge bouquet of daisies. As she handed the flowers to Josie, she could see her family and friends standing in the front row and beaming proudly in her direction.

Maybe it didn't matter that she hadn't gotten first place, after all. She had worked hard, performed beautifully, and had the time of her life!

"I don't need a trophy at all," Josie thought to herself as she smiled back proudly at her loved ones.

Three New Things

Mia wasn't afraid to try new things. In fact, she loved trying new things. Even if it was something unfamiliar, or hard, or even a little scary, Mia still wanted to give it a shot. She was always up for the next big adventure.

Not only did Mia love to try new things, but it also didn't really bother her if she struggled, or even failed. To Mia, it wasn't about being the best at something. It was just about learning something new and having a good time while she was doing it.

One Sunday evening, as Mia was getting ready to start a new week, she made a special goal for herself. She promised herself that she would try three new things over the next week. She was so excited about the goal that she could hardly sleep that night. She awoke bright and early on Monday morning, ready to try something completely new!

As Mia was walking to school, she passed the art center downtown. She noticed a flyer hanging on the door advertising a ceramics class. The class was that afternoon at 4:00. Perfect! Mia would have time to make it to the class right after school was out, and ceramics was something that she'd never tried before.

When the final bell rang, Mia rushed over to the art center just in time to start the class.

The ceramics instructor, Mr. Tom, started by handing everyone in the class a big, lumpy, grey ball of clay. Mia was excited! She couldn't wait to turn this clay into something beautiful!

Mr. Tom showed everyone in class how to put the clay on a potter's wheel and then spin the wheel around and around while shaping the clay into a tall, slender vase.

Mr. Tom made it look so easy, but every time that Mia tried, her clay collapsed into a messy pile on the wheel.

Mia didn't give up. She tried and tried and tried, but no matter what she did, she couldn't get the clay to cooperate. When she glanced at the clock, she saw that there were only five minutes left of the class. There was no way she was going to finish the vase, but she still didn't give up. She quickly took the clay off the wheel and used her hand to shape it into a small shallow bowl.

Mr. Tom glanced at Mia's work.

"What do you have there, Mia?" Mr. Tom asked in a friendly, but curious voice.

"Well, I was having a really hard time with the vase, so I made a milk dish for my cat, Jiggles. Do you think she'll like it?'

"I sure do," said Mr. Tom. "And I like the way you think.

"Thanks!" said Mia with a smile.

"One new thing down, two to go!" Mia thought to herself as she made her way home with Jiggle's new milk dish.

When Mia awoke on Wednesday morning, fluffy white snowflakes were falling outside of her window. It was the first real snow of the season. It made Mia feel happy on the inside. It also gave her a perfect idea for a second new thing to try.

Ice skating! Mia had never been ice skating before and the ice-skating rink at the community center always opened for the season on the same day as the first snowfall. She was excited to give it a try.

That evening, after Mia had finished her homework, she asked to borrow her mother's old ice skates.

"Are you going ice skating, Mia?" asked her mother. "But you don't even know how."

"That's alright, Mom. I can learn!" replied Mia excitedly.

"Have fun and be careful," said Mia's mother as she handed her an old pair of ice skates.

Mia wandered slowly down the sidewalk to the ice-skating rink, admiring the dazzling, white drifts of snow on the city streets.

When she finally made it to the busy rink, she tied on the skates and wobbled out onto the ice.

As soon as she hit the ice, she fell flat on her bottom. It didn't bother Mia. She got back up and tried again. And again, she fell down. This time, she fell right on top of someone else.

"Oh goodness! I'm so sorry!" Mia said as she scrambled up off of the ice.

"That's okay. Are you alright?" asked the young girl that Mia had knocked down. She was just about Mia's age.

"I'm fine. What about you?" replied Mia.

"I'm okay, too," answered the other girl. "My name is Kara, by the way. Have you ever ice skated before?"

"Nope!' said Mia. "Does it show?"

"Kind of. Do you want me to show you?" asked Kara.

"That would be great!" exclaimed Mia.

"Let's do it!" Kara said as she took Mia's hand and helped her around the ice.

Soon, Mia was skating all by herself. And—she had made a new friend!

"Two new things down, one to go!" Mia thought to herself as she walked home later that night in the chilly air with the skates flung over her shoulder.

The rest of the week passed quickly. Before Mia knew it, Saturday morning had arrived. She still had one more, new thing to try if she wanted to meet her goal. But what?

She made her way to the kitchen to make herself some toast, trying to think of something new that she could try.

"Sorry, Sweetie," said her father when he saw her rummaging around in the cabinets, "I just ate the last piece of bread with my morning coffee."

"That's it!" Mia thought to herself. She had never made bread before! Baking bread would be her third new thing for the week!

Mia flipped through her mother's recipe books searching for the perfect recipe. There were so many to choose from, but she finally settled on a recipe that didn't seem too complicated.

She tried to follow the recipe as best she could, but there wasn't quite enough flour in the cupboard, and she may have added just a little too much milk. Mia mixed it up all the same, dumped the dough in a big pan, and waited for it to bake.

Mia continued to flip through the recipe book as the bread baked, admiring the delicious-looking cakes and cookies on the pages. Soon, she had lost all track of time. Before long, smoke began to rise from the oven.

The bread! It was burning!

Mia rushed to the oven and pulled the burnt loaf off the rack. She placed the bread on the counter and stared at it. It certainly didn't look like the pictures of golden brown, crusty bread on the pages of the cookbook, but Mia hated to think about throwing it away.

She glanced absently out of the kitchen window, trying to figure out what to do with the bread. There, outside the window, she saw seven red birds pecking at the cold ground. Mia thought they looked hungry. So hungry, in fact, that they might just love to have some freshly baked bread!

Mia waited a little longer for the bread to cool and then broke it up into small crumbs. She quietly opened the kitchen door and approached the group of birds, gently tossing the crumbs in their direction.

The delighted birds ate the crumbs faster than Mia could toss them. Mia felt delighted, too.

"Three new things down, none to go!" Mia thought to herself as she hurried back to the warm and cozy kitchen.

Mia poured herself a cup of hot chocolate, sat down at the kitchen table, and thought back over the week she'd had.

She may not have made the most beautiful vase, but she had made Jiggles feel very special with his new milk bowl.

She may not have been the best ice skater, but she had made a new friend.

She may not have made the tastiest bread, but there were some pretty satisfied birds outside her window.

A happy cat, happy birds, and a new friend!

Goal accomplished!

Thank you for buying our book!

If you find this storybook fun and useful, I would be very grateful if you could post a short review on Amazon! Your support does make a difference and I read every review personally.

If you would like to leave a review, just head on over to this book's Amazon page and click "Write a customer review".

Thank you for your support!

Printed in Great Britain
by Amazon

70525753R00047